MW01099142

Kelsey's Candy World Adventure

by Rhonda Warnack

Illustrated by Sheilagh Foster-Hill

AuthorHouse™
1663 Liberty Drive
Bloomington, IN 47403
www.authorhouse.com
Phone: 1-800-839-8640

© 2009 Rhonda Warnack. All rights reserved.

No part of this book may be reproduced, stored in a retrieval system, or transmitted
by any means without the written permission of the author.

First published by AuthorHouse 11/13/2009

ISBN: 978-1-4490-4438-1 (sc)

Library of Congress Control Number: 2009912050

Printed in the United States of America
Bloomington, Indiana

This book is printed on acid-free paper.

Life is
an adventure,
Live it!.
Rhonda Warnack
Dec. 2009

One day when Kelsey was seven years old, her mother and father told her they were going on an amazing voyage around the world in a big, beautiful ship. They would visit many countries and meet all sorts of new people.

Kelsey was very excited but also a little scared. "Everything will be so different," she thought. "Will I meet any new friends? What will they be like? Will they like the same things we like here at home?"

While they were packing, she told her parents she was worried about everything being so new and how she would miss the things that she was used to. She would miss her friends and her dog. Then she asked, "What about my favorite candy. Do they have candy in other countries? What does it taste like?"

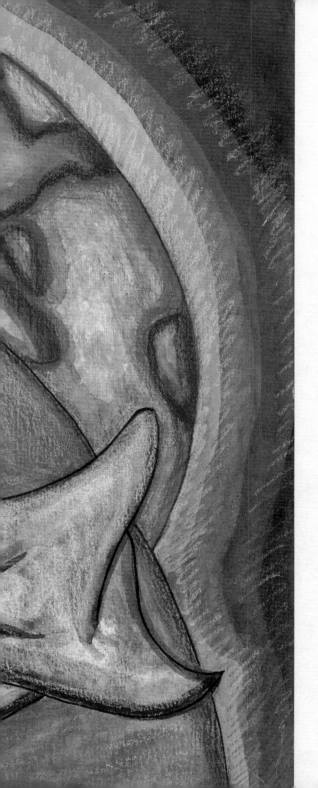

Kelsey's father hugged her and said, "As soon as we get back, you'll see your friends and Scruffy again. And as for candy, kids are the same all around the world. They all like candy." Then he came up with a great idea. "Why don't we try new candies in all the countries and find your favorite?"

Kelsey thought about this and decided she would find the best candy in the entire world. Now she was very excited to be on her candy world adventure.

Their first stop was Puerto Rico. As soon as they got into town, Kelsey and her mom found a candy stand. Although the candy man only spoke a little English, Kelsey quickly learned how to explain her candy adventure to others. He helped her pick out some candy he thought she would like.

"This candy bar is Sabrosita," the man said "Made from sweet milk and guava. Also try seeded ginger cookies. They are made from sugar molasses and ginger. These are my daughter's favorites."

Kelsey was so excited she couldn't wait to start trying the candy. She tried the guava bar first. "It's okay," she told her mother. "I like the guava part."

She liked the last candy the best—the ginger seed cookies. After trying them, Kelsey said, "Yum! The ginger cookies taste like toffee and popcorn." Kelsey had found her favorite candy from Puerto Rico. She thought about the candy man and remembered that he said his daughter liked this one the best too.

Although Kelsey really liked Puerto Rico, she couldn't wait to get to their next stop, Salvador, Brazil, and try some of their candy. Like Puerto Rico, Kelsey and her parents found a candy cart and a nice man who told them all about Brazilian candy.

He thought for awhile and said, "Oh yes, you must also try, Baton which is made of chocolate." He also suggested they try a licorice made from molasses. "But the most popular in Salvador is Bala de Goma, which is a fruit-flavored jelly candy," he said. They thanked the man for all of his help and headed back for the ship.

Puerto Rico

By this time, Kelsey had made some new friends on the ship. They were all about her age. She thought it would be fun if they would help her with her candy treasure hunt.

First, they tried the chocolaty Baton candy bar. Kelsey took one bite. "It's too crumbly. But it is chocolaty," they all said.

Finally, they tried the two kinds of jelly candies. The girls liked the molasses candy, but the boys said, "It's too much like syrup, not like licorice." The last candy to taste was the Balas De Goma. "This is great," Mike said. "I like the orange."

"I like the green," commented Calvin. But they all agreed the Balas De Goma fruit jellies were their favorites. Kelsey's mother reminded Kelsey, "This is one of the most popular candies in Salvador too."

There were many reasons to be excited about their next port, Cape Town, South Africa. Kelsey was going on a safari to see lions, zebras, and giraffes. She was also continuing her adventure into the world of candies.

Kelsey's parents found a candy store in a mall. Kelsey picked out three kinds of candy the store owner told her were good. Her first choice was sour-colored worms that looked like colorful sugar-covered jelly worms. Second were the chocolate bullets, which were chocolate-covered black licorice. And finally, she chose the most unusual, candy apricots, which were apricot foam covered with chocolate.

South
Africa
Capetown

"I like the sour worms." Mike said. "They're really sour and they stay sour."

"Yeah." agreed Kelsey and Laura. "The worms are fun and they make my mouth pucker."

Next they tried the apricot candy. "It tastes like soap." muttered Calvin.

"Oh my gosh, it tastes like apricots." replied Laura, "but it's too sweet."

"I like the chocolate bullets. They're great." said Mike "We don't have anything like this at home." Calvin said.

"But I don't like licorice." responded Laura. So they all agreed that the sour worms were their favorite.

Later that night Kelsey told her mom, "It's funny. All my new friends are from the United States, but we don't always like the same candy. I bet the kids from all these other countries don't always agree either."

They were on the ship for a long time before they got to India. Kelsey couldn't wait to get back to her candy adventure. Her mother took her to a store where they had lots of candy. Kelsey chose two that that she thought looked good. They were both hard candies that the store clerk said were very popular. One was strawberry cream, and the other was a caramel toffee.

Again, the four tried the candies to see which one was best. "They're both okay," said Mike.

"Yeah, I really like the strawberry kind," agreed Laura.

"But they taste like candy at home," said Calvin.

"Yeah, I bet kids here like the same kind of stuff we do," said Kelsey.

Kelsey was dreaming about getting to their next stop. It was a small island called Mauritius. There they could go swimming, see amazing fish, and play on the beach. While she was there, Kelsey met a girl named Ashana who showed her all of her favorite candies. Ashana's favorite was a spongy jelly made from a swirl of marshmallow and jelly, and her sister's was Tamarind, a candy made from herbs.

When she got back to the ship, Kelsey shared her candies with her ship friends. First, they tried the spongy jelly. "I like the spongy part," said Calvin.

"I like the jelly part," said Laura.

"It's all good," Mike said with his mouth full.

Then they tried the Tamarind. "Yuck. It tastes like medicine," said Calvin and Mike.

The girls tried it and said, "It's okay, but not our favorites." They agreed the spongy jelly was one of their all-time favorites. "That's just what Ashana thought too," Kelsey told them.

There were only two ports to go, and Kelsey was realizing that candy wasn't all that different around the world. When they got to China, Kelsey found many different kinds of jelly candy. With the help from some kids at a candy store, Kelsey picked out three of the most popular jelly candies. She chose pineapple, orange, and strawberry jellies.

The four adventurers tasted the jellies. "The orange doesn't really taste like anything," Kelsey said.

"But the pineapple really tastes like pineapple!" exclaimed Calvin.

Both Laura and Mike agreed. But the one that was the best to all of them was the strawberry. "It tastes like my favorite candy at home," Laura squealed.

When the trip started, Kelsey was so nervous she wouldn't like living on a ship, making new friends, and trying new candies. Now that they had only one port left, Kelsey knew these were all great things and she would miss the ship, her new friends, and especially trying new candies. So when Kelsey and her dad looked for candy in Japan, she wanted to make sure she chose something extra special.

She talked with adults and kids at a grocery store and asked them to help her choose candy for her friends. They helped her pick out a bag of assorted chocolate candies that were flavored with caramel, white chocolate, green tea, and cookies. She also chose a candy called Tengudo, which was a molasses candy wrapped in rice paper.

Mike, Calvin, and Laura were very excited to see what Kelsey chose for them from Japan. They all tried different kinds of chocolates. "This one is the best ever," mumbled Calvin as he ate a caramel chocolate.

"I don't like this one at all," said Laura. "My candy is green." Then they all tried the others and found their favorite.

"It's different than candy bar chocolate at home but it's still good," replied Kelsey

Finally, they tried the Tengudo. Kelsey's mom explained that the rice paper around the molasses was part of the candy and was very good. So, all four tried the candy, paper and all. They all chewed for a while when Calvin explained, "If you eat just the rice paper, it's really good." Everyone laughed, but they all agreed. They liked the rice paper most of all. "It's just like they said at the store," replied Kelsey.

CARAMEL CHOCOLATE

When they finished with the candies from Japan, Kelsey's mom asked them to remember their very favorites. "I liked the sour worms from South Africa," answered Mike.

"I can't decide between the spongy jellies in Mauritius and the strawberry jellies from China," Laura told them.

"My favorite candy was the different fruit jellies from Brazil," said Calvin.

"I liked so many of them, but I guess my favorite was the chocolate candies from Japan," remembered Kelsey.

That evening after dinner, Kelsey and her parents were talking about the great adventure she had taken. Her father asked, "Out of all those candies, why do you think the chocolate candies were your favorite?" Kelsey thought about this for a long time. Finally, she answered, "I guess because they were all different but still the same. Just like all the people we have met on this trip."

This made Kelsey start to think. There were kids all over the world who liked candy that she liked. "Maybe kids around the world aren't so different."

Kelsey realized that she found an even better treasure than the world's best candy. She found out that all over world kids were very much like her.